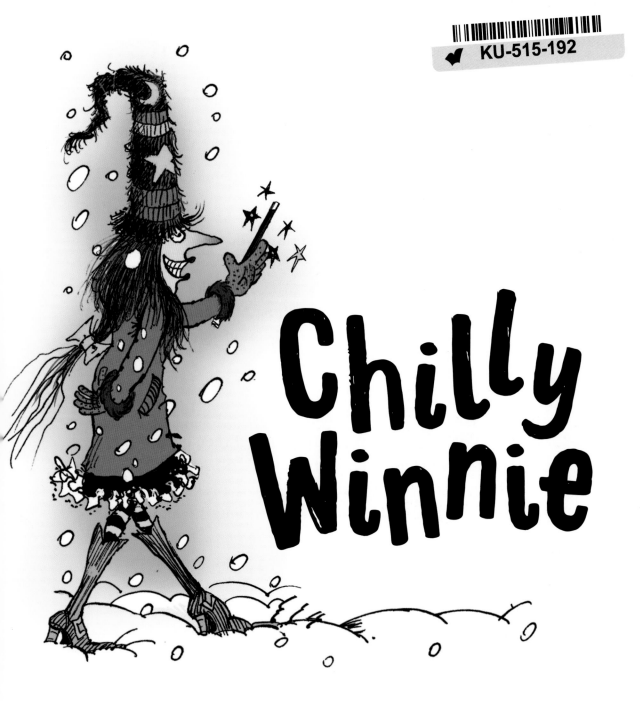

Chilly Winnie

LAURA OWEN & KORKY PAUL

OXFORD
UNIVERSITY PRESS

Helping your child to read

Before they start

- ★ Can your child remember a snowy day? Talk about what it's like going out in the snow.
- ★ Read the back cover blurb with your child. Explain that 'abominable' means 'terrible'. What do they think Winnie's abominable snowman would be like?

During reading

- ★ Let your child read at their own pace – don't worry if it's slow. Offer them plenty of help if they get stuck, and enjoy the story together.
- ★ Help them to work out words they don't know by saying each sound out loud and then blending them to say the word, e.g. *a-b-o-m-i-n-a-b-l-e, abominable*.
- ★ If your child still struggles with a word, just tell them the word and move on.
- ★ Give them lots of praise for good reading!

After reading

- ★ Look at page 48 for some fun activities.

Contents

OXFORD
UNIVERSITY PRESS

Great Clarendon Street, Oxford OX2 6DP
Oxford University Press is a department of the University of Oxford.
It furthers the University's objective of excellence in research, scholarship,
and education by publishing worldwide. Oxford is a registered trade mark
of Oxford University Press in the UK and in certain other countries

"Abominable Winnie" was first published in *Winnie Takes the Plunge* 2011
"Woolly Wilbur" was first published in *Winnie Goes Wild* 2013

This edition published 2020

British Library Cataloguing in Publication Data

Data available

ISBN: 978-0-19-277374-6

1 3 5 7 9 10 8 6 4 2

Printed in China

Paper used in the production of this book is a natural,
recyclable product made from wood grown in sustainable forests.
The manufacturing process conforms to the environmental
regulations of the country of origin.

Acknowledgements
With thanks to Caterine Baker for editorial support.

Abominable Winnie

Winnie looked out of the window. "Yippee-dippee, Wilbur!" she yelled. "It's snowing!"

She rushed down to the kitchen. "We need a nice warm breakfast," she said. "How about snail slime porridge?"

"Meeow!" said Wilbur.

"This porridge smells abominable!" said Winnie.
"People have told me that my cooking is abominable –
so it must mean really, really nice!"

Wilbur shook his head, but Winnie didn't notice.

After breakfast, Winnie and Wilbur put on their hats, gloves and tail warmers. They went outside for a walk in the snow.

Brrrrrr! Brrrrrr! Brrrrrr!
Splot!

Winnie flopped back into the snow. She made a witch-shaped print.

Splat!

Wilbur made a cat-shaped print, and added twigs for whiskers.

"Come on, Wilbur!" shouted Winnie. "Let's have an abominable snowball fight!"

Before long, there were snowballs flying everywhere.

"Tee hee!" laughed Winnie. "Splat on the cat!"

Then Wilbur scooped up a really big snowball, and threw it.

Pheew-plop! It went right down Winnie's neck.

slip, slide, slip.

"Urrgh!" shivered Winnie. "I've had enough of snowball fights. What shall we do now?"

Then Winnie spotted some children making a snowman. "Let's go and help, Wilbur!" she said.

They all worked together, and soon they had made a brilliant snow witch.

"How abominable!" said Winnie.

Just then, Winnie had an idea. "I can make a snowman that's even more abominable than that!" she said.

"Abracadabra!"

"Uh-oh," said the children. "What's that?"

"It's a lovely abominable snowman, of course!" said Winnie.

Gulp! went the children. The abominable snowman was

huge!

It was hairy, and it was walking towards them. It didn't look at all friendly!

The abominable snowman
started chasing the children.
Wilbur tried to stop
the snowman, but it
tripped over him.
It rolled down
the hill, faster
and faster!
Soon it
looked like a
giant
snowball.

"Abra—"

began Winnie.

But then the giant snowball

rolled over her.

Splat!

Gulp!

17

The snowball rolled on down the hill, with Winnie inside it! It started to pick up the children, too.

"Stop that!" shouted Mrs Parmar from the school. But the snowball didn't stop. It picked up Mrs Parmar, too!

Finally, the snowball
reached the bottom of the hill.
Thump! At last it stopped.
Winnie grabbed her wand.
"Abracadabra!"

19

Puffff! The abominable snowball vanished.
Everyone landed softly in the snow.

Then Winnie had a fantastic idea! "Let's make
a really **big** snowball!" she said.

"No!" said Mrs Parmar. "We've all had enough of big snowballs."

"Not that kind of snowball!" laughed Winnie.

"I mean a Snow Ball – a big posh party, with dancing!"

Mrs Parmar was just about to say it was
impossible . . . when Winnie waved her wand.

"Abracadabra!"

Suddenly, there was a beautiful igloo, just right for a party!

Winnie waved her wand again. At once, everyone was dressed up for the Snow Ball. There was food. And balloons. And a band was playing!

23

So everyone ate and danced and sang until it was time to go home.

"That was an abominable party!" said Winnie happily.

"No, it wasn't!" said Mrs Parmar. "Abominable means terrible!"

"Oh!" said Winnie. "So when people said my cooking was abominable, they meant it was . . ."

"*Interesting*," said Mrs Parmar. "Thank you for a wonderful party, Winnie!"

Woolly Wilbur

Winnie woke up with a frozen nose. Her teeth were chattering like tap-dancing skeletons.

Winnie got dressed fast, then she and Wilbur
hurried downstairs.

"I know what we need, Wilbur,"
she said. "A nice big mug of
hot chocolate!"

But when she opened
the fridge . . .

. . . there was no milk!

"Oh, newts' knees, Wilbur!" said Winnie.

"We'll have to go to the shops and get some!"

It was snowing outside, so Wilbur opened the cupboard to get their woollies.

But out flew five fat clothes moths.

They had eaten all the warm clothes!

"We can't go out there without our woollies, Wilbur!" said Winnie. "I'll just have to knit us some more."

But when she opened the wool cupboard, there was nothing in it except more clothes moths.

"You greedy, gobbling moths!" yelled Winnie.
"You've eaten all my wool! Now how are we going
to stay warm on our way to the shops?"

Suddenly, Winnie had a good idea.

"I know how to get wool!" she shouted. "We need a flock of fat, fluffy sheep! **Abracadabra!**"

Nothing happened. So Winnie and Wilbur went outside to see if the sheep were waiting there.

"Waddling wombats!" said Winnie. "No sheep – but look at the size of those snowflakes!"

Thump! Wilbur jumped out of the way just in time.

A sheep nearly landed on him.

Thump!

Thump! More and more sheep landed.

"Come in! Come in!" said Winnie to the sheep.

"Shut the door, Wilbur, and let's get clipping!"

Soon Winnie and Wilbur had clipped most of the wool off the sheep.

"We need to spin the wool before I can knit it," said Winnie. "I know who's good at spinning – spiders! **Abracadabra!**"

Soon a group of spiders was busy spinning the wool.

Wilbur helped Winnie to wind the wool.

"I'll knit as fast as I can, Wilbur!" she said.

"I can't wait to drink a big, bubbling mug of

hot chocolate!"

Winnie grabbed two broom handles and started knitting. Knit, knit. Clickety-click.

But the knitting was too big.

"This tail warmer will never fit you, Wilbur!" Winnie groaned.

So Winnie tried knitting with wands instead.

Knit, knit. Clickety-click.

That was much better! Soon she had a lovely pile of hats, gloves and tail warmers.

Winnie and Wilbur put on all their new woollies.

But when Winnie opened the door, there was a huge pile of snow blocking their way.

"Slithering slugs!" said Winnie. "How will we ever get to the shops now?"

Winnie and Wilbur tried digging the snow away,

but it was very deep.

Then, Winnie had another idea. She made a catapult out of all the too-big knitting.

Then she popped Wilbur in the catapult and fired him off towards the shops.

"Meeeoooooow!" complained Wilbur, as he flew

through the air.

Flump!

He landed just outside the shop.

"That looks fun!" said all the children.

Wilbur got the milk, and then the children helped him dig a path back home.

When they got there, all the children took turns to be catapulted into the snow. **Flump!**

And Winnie made a big cauldron of hot chocolate
for everyone to share.

Yum!

After reading activities

Talk about the stories

Ask your child the following questions. Encourage them to talk about their answers.

1) In "Abominable Winnie", what does the abominable snowman do?

2) Would you like to be at the Snow Ball party in "Abominable Winnie"? Why?

3) In "Woolly Wilbur", how does Wilbur get home from the shop?

1) Chases everyone and rolls them up into a snowball; 2) Open – child's own opinion; 3) The children help him dig a path back through the snow.

Try this!

What tasty treats do you think everyone would eat at the Snow Ball? Write and draw a menu.